W9-AMC-982

Fly, Firefly!

Written by Shana Keller

Illustrated by Ramona Kaulitzki

On a breeze, through the trees,

a wind current carried him out

to see the sea.

Now he was farther than he meant to be.

To the left he ebbed.

To the right he flowed.

He saw the sparkles that flashed and glowed.

He dove and splashed through the wet glass,

but under the surface, air did not last.

My niece and I saw him sink into the sea.

His poor little wings couldn't break free.

The sea pushed and tugged
while I scooped up our bug.

"Little firefly,"
Marjie said.
"It's not flies that you see!"

"That's bioluminescence swirling

and twirling through the great sea!"

"You are way off track,
but we'll carry you back."

"Trust us, you'll see.
That glittering there is from the sea.

That glowing HERE is your own family."

"Fly, firefly! Fly toward the trees."

"Stay closer this time to your real family."

About Rachel Carson

The idea for this story came from a letter I read, a letter Rachel Carson wrote to her friend Dorothy Freeman about an encounter with a firefly. Around midnight, Rachel and her niece headed down to the shore to secure their family raft. Once on the shore, they turned their flashlights off and saw a sea filled with "diamonds and emeralds." Rachel joked how one of them took to the air. She soon realized it was a firefly who "thought" the flashes in the water were signals from other fireflies and hastened to rescue him.

It was one of those experiences that gives an odd and hard-to-describe feeling, with so many overtones beyond the facts themselves. I have never seen any account scientifically, of fireflies responding to other phosphorescence. . . . And I've already thought of a child's story based on it—but maybe that will never get written.
(*Always, Rachel: The Letters of Rachel Carson and Dorothy Freeman, 1952-1964; page 187*)

As far as we know, Rachel never completed this project. However, in July 1956, she published an article in *Woman's Home Companion* titled, "Help Your Child to Wonder." Filled with her own sense of wonder, Rachel, a scientist and author, believed in protecting the environment. She wrote several scientific books about the world around us, including *Under the Sea-Wind: A Naturalist's Picture of Ocean Life*, *The Sea Around Us*, and *The Edge of the Sea*. But it wasn't until Rachel received a letter from another friend, Olga Owens Huckins, about the birds dying on her land—land that was sprayed with pesticides—that drove Rachel to write *Silent Spring*, one of the most impactful books of our century.

Published in 1962, *Silent Spring* launched what many consider to be the start of the environmental movement. In April 1963, Rachel gave an interview on *CBS Reports* to share her concerns for the environment directly with the public. A month later, she was called before Congress to testify. Rachel defended her research in *Silent Spring* despite harassment from government officials and chemical companies. Thanks to her intense investigation of the chemicals used to kill bugs, the government finally began to regulate the use of pesticides. Consequently, many federal and state laws were created to protect our air, land, water, and endangered species.

Though Rachel died in 1964, only two years after *Silent Spring* was released, her book sparked a worldwide environmental movement that continues to this day.

"In nature nothing exists alone." —Rachel Carson, *Silent Spring*

Living Light

Insects dominate our planet. They were the first animals that learned how to fly. They have been around for nearly 500 million years and are an integral part of our planet's health. Beetles form the largest group of insects, of which more than 2,000 species of fireflies have been classified. Their name might be confusing, but fireflies are not actually flies. They are beetles that can fly. Every firefly blinks its own pattern, or rhythm, to communicate. Although beetles don't live in the ocean, most fireflies like to live near water, such as rivers and lakes. Like people, fireflies can see in color.

The glittering light from the ocean, though often referred to as phosphorescence, is actually bioluminescence. Bioluminescence is the result of a natural chemical reaction that occurs in certain organisms, creating an effect we often see as flashing or glowing light. Some people call this living light.

Most bioluminescent organisms live in the ocean. Based on her location, the bioluminescence Rachel and the firefly saw probably came from a form of marine plankton (single-celled microscopic plants) called dinoflagellates. Their flashing light occurs when the organism is disturbed or stimulated by breaking waves, other animals, humans, passing boats, and even rainfall. Dinoflagellates live on the surface, while other bioluminescent creatures, like the anglerfish, live at the bottom of the ocean. Only a handful—including certain fireflies, glowworms, millipedes, and mushrooms—live on land.

Bioluminescence is often confused with fluorescence and phosphorescence. The difference is that bioluminescence is caused by a chemical reaction. Fluorescence occurs when a short wavelength of light is absorbed by an object and then a longer wavelength of light is emitted. Highlighter pens and markers and the reflective parts of road signs are a result of fluorescence. Phosphorescence is related to fluorescence; however, it does not instantly reemit the light it has absorbed. Glow sticks and glow-in-the-dark items are a result of phosphorescent materials.

Bioluminescent chemistry is a fairly new subject. Many scientists are discovering new ways to use this natural technology. Some are developing bioluminescent trees in an effort to light cities up at night. Others are experimenting with plants that light up to alert farmers when their crops need food, water, or are ready for harvest.

For every child who sees the wonders in the world.

—Shana

For Julian

—Ramona

I'd like to thank Jeanne Cecil, Executive Director of the Rachel Carson Homestead in Springdale, Pennsylvania; Clyde Sorenson, professor of Entomology at North Carolina State University; and Kristen Hunter-Cevera, Hibbitt Early Career Fellow at the Marine Biological Laboratory, for answering all of my questions and sharing not just their knowledge but their enthusiasm as well.

More information about Rachel's historic home can be found at rachelcarsonhomestead.org.

—Shana

Text Copyright © 2020 Shana Keller
Illustration Copyright © 2020 Ramona Kaulitzki
Design Copyright © 2020 Sleeping Bear Press

All rights reserved. No part of this book may be reproduced in any manner without the express written consent of the publisher, except in the case of brief excerpts in critical reviews and articles. All inquiries should be addressed to:

SLEEPING BEAR PRESS™

2395 South Huron Parkway, Suite 200
Ann Arbor, MI 48104
www.sleepingbearpress.com

Printed and bound in the United States.

10 9 8 7 6 5 4 3 2 1 (hardcover)
10 9 8 7 6 5 4 3 2 (paperback)

Library of Congress Cataloging-in-Publication Data

Names: Keller, Shana, 1977- author. | Kaulitzki, Ramona, illustrator.
Title: Fly, firefly / written by Shana Keller ; illustrated by Ramona Kaulitzki.
Description: Ann Arbor, MI : Sleeping Bear Press, 2020. | Audience: Ages 4-8. | Summary: Illustrations and easy-to-read, rhyming text show how a firefly that has been confused by bioluminescence in the ocean is helped by two humans to find its family on shore.
Identifiers: LCCN 2019036854 | ISBN 9781534110335 (hardcover) | ISBN 9781534111097 (paperback)
Subjects: CYAC: Stories in rhyme. | Fireflies—Fiction. | Bioluminescence—Fiction.
Classification: LCC PZ8.3.K2945 Fly 2020 | DDC [E]—dc23
LC record available at https://lccn.loc.gov/2019036854

Firefly Photo © khlungcenter /Shutterstock.com